EJ   Schachner, Judith
            Byron.

            Willy and May.

14
DAY
BOOK

DATE			

WITHDRAWN

Willy and May

Judith Byron Schachner

DUTTON CHILDREN'S BOOKS ◆ New York

Library of Congress Cataloging-in-Publication Data

Schachner, Judith Byron.
Willy and May/by Judith Byron Schachner.—1st ed.
p.   cm.
Summary: A girl who always looks forward to her visits with
her Great-aunt May and May's canary Willy is terribly disappointed
when she thinks she will not be able to see them one Christmas.
ISBN 0-525-45347-4
[1. Great-aunts—Fiction. 2. Canaries—Fiction. 3. Christmas—Fiction.]
I. Title.
PZ7.S3286Wi   1995   [E]—dc20   94-43785   CIP   AC

Published in the United States 1995 by Dutton Children's Books,
a division of Penguin Books USA Inc.
375 Hudson Street, New York, New York 10014
Designed by Amy Berniker
Printed in Hong Kong
First Edition
1 3 5 7 9 10 8 6 4 2

For
Dad and Eileen
with Love

My Great-Aunt May lived her whole life in a small white cottage by some very tall pine trees. It was a long trip from our house to hers, so we got to visit only twice a year — once in the summertime and once at Christmas. I loved May very much.

May lived alone in the house with her bird, Willy. Willy was small and yellow and — more often than not — could be found sitting on top of May's fuzzy gray hair.

May was small and bony with quick, sparkly eyes. She looked very much like a bird herself, flitting about the house in her flowery dresses.

May never had children of her own, so Willy became her special fellow. And I was her special girl. Willy loved May more than anyone, but he was always excited to see me.

When I walked through May's front door, Willy zoomed to the top of my head. He trilled a cheerful tune in the hope of receiving an egg biscuit from my hand. But Willy wasn't always so polite.

May's heart was as big as a full moon, and every stray animal that happened along was attracted to its light. Dogs, cats, raccoons, squirrels — May fed them all. Willy just turned his back on the scruffy crew and stuck an indignant beak into the air.

On summer mornings, May loved to take Willy for walks.
During my visits, I would join them. Everybody in town knew
the lady with the bird on her head. They were practically famous.
Mr. Carlos, the grocer, always had a cracker for the "leedle" bird.
Mrs. Larson, the baker, made canary cookies sprinkled with yellow
sugar. May always bought dozens of them and passed them out to
the children we met. People pointed and waved at us. Willy and I
loved the attention.

May always took her butterfly net with her, in case a stiff wind
blew Willy off her hat. She let me carry it when we went to town.
One day, Willy missed the net and landed in Mrs. Harvey's
pocketbook. He was returned to us after Mrs. Harvey found him
chirping in her change purse. May gently removed Willy from the
nickels and dimes, and she and I both gave a sigh of relief.

After our walks, it was nice to come home again. I would fill two glasses with cold lemonade while May put cucumber sandwiches on china plates. We'd sink into the old couch and watch Willy perform. The door to Willy's cage was always open. He was free to fly everywhere because May knew he would never fly away.

Sometimes he swooped loopity-loops over our heads, and once he flew straight into a wall. May made an ice pack and tenderly placed it on his tiny head.

Saturdays were for baking. The smell of spices filled the old
kitchen. May taught me to make the best apple pies. She would
put her hands on mine and we'd roll out a fine crust and carefully
place the dough on a mountain of apples. Then we would let Willy
dance all over the top, pressing his birdy feet into the soft dough.
On Sunday we ate the goodies.

"Singing after supper is good for one's digestion," May always
said. She'd put a record on the old Victrola and we'd sing along
while we did the dishes. Willy would ride the records around and
around, chirping and spinning until he became so dizzy he fell
headfirst into May's knitting basket.

Summer afternoons, we went berry picking. May would put on her old straw hat with the papier-mâché cherries. Willy would sit on top, pecking at the make-believe fruit. By the time our baskets were filled to the brim, the sun was hot, and May and I would swim in the pond.

Once she kicked off her shoes and walked, still wearing her
clothes, straight into the water until she disappeared, leaving Willy
and her hat to float on top.

Moments later, she popped up and said, "Care to join me?" as if
she had done nothing unusual. So, of course, I jumped right in.

In the winter, we decorated May's tree. She brought the dusty boxes down from the attic, and I carefully unwrapped and hung the fancy old ornaments, one by one. Then May handed me a needle and thread to string cranberry and marshmallow garlands. Willy decorated, too. He added dust bunnies and lint, lost bobby pins and birdseed.

May would adjust a light or move an icicle. Then it was perfect.
I wouldn't have missed that moment for the world.

And so it went, summer and winter, year after year. But one year it looked as though I might miss it all. During the summer, Mom became ill. This meant we couldn't visit Willy and May. May didn't drive, and no one could take me on the long trip to their house. Dad said, "Cheer up. Christmas will be here before you know it." I didn't want to cry in front of Mom, so I went to my room.

I wanted Mom to get better, and also wanted to see Willy and
May. I missed them so much. We wrote to each other often, filling
our letters with hugs and kisses. Willy stamped his inky feet all
over the envelopes.

By December, Mom was better but still needed my help at home.
I wrote and told May that we couldn't come for Christmas. My tears
turned my words into blue puddles and made my letter hard to read.
But I knew May would understand.

One very cold week later, the mailman brought a card from May.
It read:

SET A PLACE FOR WILLY AND ME AT YOUR CHRISTMAS TABLE.

WE WILL BRING THE PLUM PUDDING! WILLY SENDS HIS CHIRPS.

LOVE, *Aunt May*

Later, while I made paper snowflakes sprinkled with glitter, Dad went out and bought the biggest Christmas tree he could find. I could hardly wait. May and Willy were really coming.

On the day before Christmas, it began to snow. By late Christmas
Eve, the winds blew hard. Snow drifted high on the empty streets.
The voice on the radio said that it was the biggest storm in years.
All the trains had stopped, and the roads were blocked. I knew May
and Willy could not come.

I pressed my nose against the frozen window and cried and cried
until I fell asleep right where I was.

It was almost dawn when I woke up, cramped with cold. From outside I could hear the muffled sound of bells and a man's laughter. When I looked down into the frozen street, I saw not a man but an old woman with a bird on her head.

I flew downstairs as May peeked around the front door.

The wind blew Willy in over my head, and I spun around to
watch him somersault through the air. May followed us into the
hallway, where she set down Willy's cage and the plum pudding
and stamped the snow off her feet.

She took off her boots and set them side by side on the rug. Then she moved to the fireplace and wiggled her toes in front of the fire. "Well, now, this is real cozy," she said, and sat down.

"How did you get here?" I asked in astonishment.

"Oh," May said calmly, "the dearest old fellow, all tinkly with bells and smelling of balsam, offered us a ride."

"A ride?" I asked. My eyes grew wider. Willy darted to May's head and peeked over her curls.

"Oh, yes," May continued. "His sleigh was overflowing with packages, so we had to squeeze in. But he didn't seem to mind. He just laughed and laughed."

"Who was he?" I asked.

May cocked her head to one side in puzzlement. "I know he must have told me, but now isn't that just like me," she said. "I can't remember his name." Then she chuckled and hugged me close.

As she bent her head down to mine, Willy flew back to the tree.

And he stayed there most of Christmas Day, picking at the popcorn garlands and admiring his reflection in the Christmas balls.